Reboot.EXE

Braydon Conell

Published by Braydon Conell

Copyright © 2024 Braydon Conell
All rights reserved
ISBN: 979-8-9866693-2-8

Cover illustration and design by Bailey Hansmeyer

This is a work of fiction. All names, characters, places, and incidents are used fictitiously or of the author's imagination. Any resemblence to the contrary is purely coincidental.

To Artichoke. My little writing buddy who's all grown up.

Contents

Chapter 1 1

Chapter 2 5

Chapter 3 9

Chapter 4 21

Chapter 5 37

Chapter 6 47

Chapter 7 53

Chapter 8 60

Chapter 9 68

Chapter 10 76

Chapter 11 80

Chapter 12 84

Chapter 13 89

Chapter 14 91

Contents

Chapter 1 1
Chapter 2 ....
Chapter 3 ....
Chapter 4 23
Chapter 5 32
Chapter 6 ....
Chapter 7 ....
Chapter 8 60
Chapter 9 69
Chapter 10 ....
Chapter 11 80
Chapter 12 81
Chapter 13 89
Chapter 14 ....

//map.exe

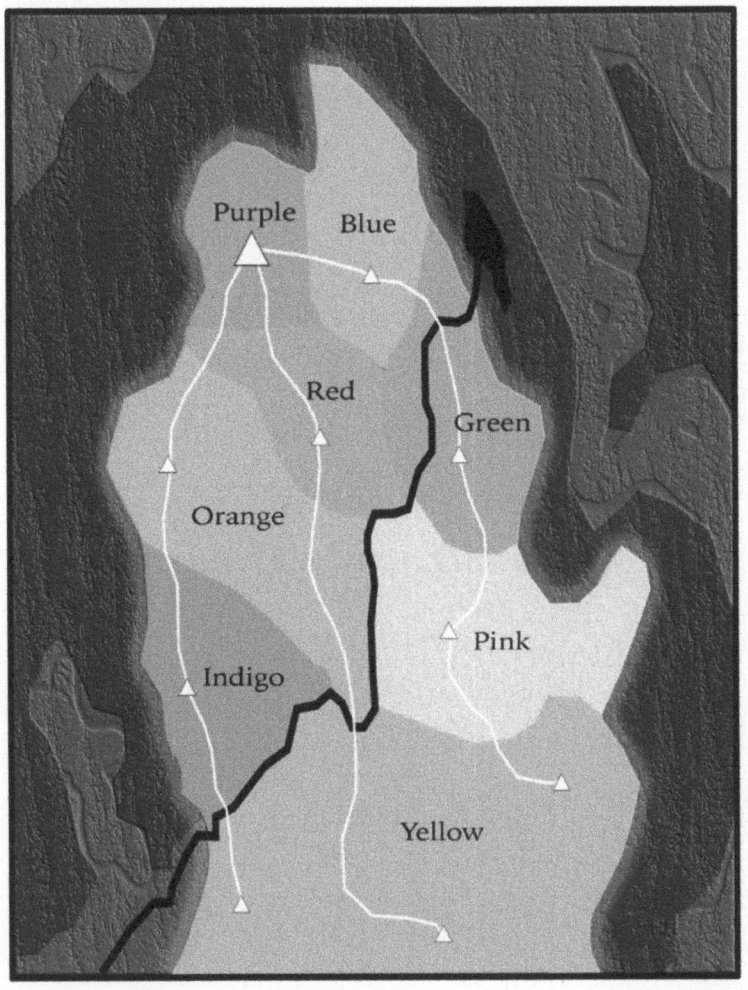

Chapter 1

Six months ago, my home came under attack. The Oasis, one of planet Earth's last remaining habitable zones, suffered under the rise of overlord Commander Balo Chu and his backers, known as Lumos. When the Machine and our Legislative Council were murdered and taken out of commission by the attack on the Tree and the plazas, the Oasis was sucked into a power vacuum. Without our leaders, Commander Chu's power went unchecked and he filled the void. Today's reality is grimmer than anything we could have imagined after the Earth Day terror.

When I set out into the fringes of the Oasis, I vowed to make it my mission to bring back the Machine, not knowing it would take this long to find him. For what has felt like ages, my team and I have been quietly and relentlessly searching the shadows for any sign of the Machine. Even just a remnant could mean we have a chance at saving our home.

After the attack on Earth Day, I was elevated, passionate, and admittedly a bit crazed at times. Now it's a laborious task to even get out of bed. No amount of sleep ever feels like enough anymore. Some days, I must fight to even continue. I hate when I feel this way, but deep down, I know I still have a purpose: save the Machine. I must press on no matter what my brain or life throws my way.

Since the attack, the Oasis has become a police state, mirroring the shackles my mind has placed on me. The wonderful haven I call home has been dismantled down to its core. However, Chu knows there is a growing resistance since Lumos isn't as popular as they believed it would be. There wasn't widespread dissent regarding how life operated in the Oasis; the people loved the Machine and the security, prosperity, and peace that he provided. In contrast, Chu only offers terror, curfews, and a lack of technology and progress. I try not to let this get to me, yet I feel I've lost everything in the overthrow, as do many others.

We are currently out on the edge of Yellow searching for the Machine. If he is alive, then surely he would be nowhere near the core of the Oasis. It would be too easy for Lumos to find the Machine there. So far, though, we have had no luck in our search either. He has hidden himself well.

The days are growing bleaker, even as I try to hold on to hope. I don't know if it's because I'm slowly losing my mind searching the outskirts of the Oasis or if there is no promise of returning to how life was with the Machine. The emptiness of the outer regions of the Oasis mirrors the numbness I feel in my heart.

"You have your worrying face on again," Ambrose says, placing his hand over my thigh. His touch always calms me even in the toughest moments.

"I know I do," I sigh. "I can't get out of my head. Every moment of my day feels like impending doom at my doorstep. It's exhausting!"

"It will work out, Luca," Ambrose wraps me into a side hug. We are sitting in the back of the van crammed in with other people, so the embrace is slightly uncomfortable, yet still strangely soothing to me.

"What's that up ahead?" I ask after noticing something glinting on the horizon.

"Just looks like some solar panels?" Marc Jensen replies from the front seat. Marc is one of my grandmother's colleagues. I've known him for several years but this mission is the most time I've spent with the man in my life. Until recently, I didn't know that he was an integral part of my grandmother's secret group, either.

"No, to the left of the panel. The sun is reflecting off something right on the horizon."

"Oh, I see it," Marc says, raising his binoculars to his eyes. He begins searching the horizon for the source of the glint. "Looks like a person. Are they flashing us?"

As we inch closer, the glint grows brighter and more blinding. At one point, the light flashes directly into my eyes, forcing my vision into nothingness. That person is definitely trying to get our attention.

"I say we head in that direction. Can't hurt to see what they want."

"Whatever you say, Boss," says Orville Haarberg who is driving the van. "Keep an eye out, everyone, for anything suspicious."

"What do you think they want?" asks Ambrose.

"Whatever it is, I hope they can offer us some help."

Chapter 2

//memory_log_03202033_phonecall >> 00:01:30

"Amelia, where are you?"

"Ross, you know, *the place*. And you also know I can't tell you over the phone. It's just not safe," replies Amelia Juniper, balancing her cell phone in one hand and cradling her baby with her other.

"With the baby, too, I assume?"

"Well, I can't just leave him home alone!"

"Oh, Amelia, why couldn't you leave him with your mother for heaven's sake? You're clear out there all alone. What if something happens?"

"You're worrying too much, Ross. No one is going to find

us out here."

"That's exactly what I'm saying. It's too dangerous for a baby outside the city."

"Let's get back to why you called so frantically. How about that?"

"Ok, fine…I'm worried because I fear the group that attacked your lab when you were in school is still around - lurking in the shadows like a cricket you swear to hear but can't seem to find. Somehow they've made it to the Oasis."

"So you, too? My mother expressed the same concern to me just a few nights ago. At the time, I thought she was just going delusional. We were so careful. How could we not catch them in the screening process? But to hear you say the same thing…what if we made a mistake?"

"The Machine was still young; perhaps it's possible he made an error? But the most important thing now is not to dwell on the past but to be cautious about what comes next. I don't know for sure if they made it here, but if they did, we're all in danger, including the Machine, and we don't know their next move."

"I will do everything I can to protect him, Ross. And for the sake of our child."

"I know you will, Amelia. That's what scares me about you. See you soon."

With the click of the line hanging up, Amelia is alone again with her baby. She doesn't know exactly why she chose this place to come to other than that it was the perfect spot away from all the hustle and bustle of the city. Growing up playing sandbox building games, this location was the oasis in the desert, the ancient ruins in the forest for her. She had the Oasis to build with Ross, but this was her little passion project. She needed something to keep her hands busy so her mind could wander. The Oasis took too much planning. Here, she could be spontaneous.

The spot wasn't unlike that of an oasis in a desert. She was out past the start of the Yellow District, where the border between the Oasis and Calamity blurred. This area's landscape was why she and Ross chose to name it Yellow. "The land of the sun. One step forward toward the future with footing in the past, yet still never falling backward," she once told Ross. It was a symbol of the Oasis that they could never return to normalcy from Calamity but must now live with it nonetheless.

Amelia found this place while exploring before even the first ground broke on the Oasis. She knew she must make it her secret. Even Ross doesn't know how to get out here. He could probably figure it out eventually, but since everything looks so similar out in the depths of the desert, he would likely drive right past it without even realizing it.

It's a small, unassuming parcel of land, not much more than an acre, with a dense thicket of towering trees to the west that butt up against a hill ending in a cliff to the east. At its center is a small spring of the clearest natural water Amelia has ever seen.

Sometimes, Amelia wishes she lived in a different world – one where Calamity never happened, society still functioned, and the world didn't collapse in on itself. A world where she could have come to this spot and built a quiet life after graduating college. A world where she could live forever with the love of her life and her beautiful children. A world without pain. A world without hatred.

But she can't have that fantasy. Instead of that life, she's here to build a safe house that no one can find unless they are searching for it with just the precise number of clues. All this work to keep her dream alive from the evil people who wish to destroy her and the Machine.

"So here we are. Are you ready to get building, buddy?" says Amelia.

//end_memory_log_03202033_phonecall >> 00:04:57

Chapter 3

"Everybody stay in the car. It could be dangerous," says Orville. "I'll go check out the situation."

"They are just drifters, not cannibals. They can't be *that* dangerous," Marc replies.

"You can never be too safe, especially with Lumos lurking around every corner now," Orville counters.

"If you say so. At least try to not get accusatory with them, please."

Orville exits the van and disappears around the front of one of the buildings. I am instantly reminded of the "raid" we did on the Lumos hideout six months ago – the one where Samantha was shot dead. Deep down, I know Marc is right and we shouldn't fear the drifters, but dread and fear consume me as a pit forms in my stomach. Yet, there is nothing we can do but wait for Orville to return.

As we wait, I check a familiar flash out of the corner of my eye. Turns out that it wasn't intentional for the light I saw on the horizon to be flashing us. Rather, it was just the sun reflecting off a shiny metal panel constructing the roof of one of the dwellings here. The metal panel is loose causing it to flap just enough in the wind for the light to bounce around.

Scanning the rest of the community we stumbled upon, the area seems to consist of a handful of homes pieced together with varying pieces of scrap metal, cloth, and wood. In the center stands an area used as a marketplace. Off to the east of the settlement is a makeshift well.

I never considered the complexities of water usage before. Living in the more connected regions of the Oasis, I have never had to worry about water. Clean, fresh water flows from the pipes every time I twist on the tap. Out here in Yellow, though, the drifters don't have such luxury. The infrastructure here wasn't set up for how and where the drifters live, but nomads still require water access. To my knowledge, the drifters usually come to the plazas in Yellow to collect enough water to last them long periods and then head back out further into the desert.

This settlement, though, seems to have a combination system. The drifters who live here must have found water beneath the surface since they built the well. It's likely a very deep well. They also have holding tanks on trailers near the well with varying capacities. So, the well must not be enough to sustain them, but it reduces the need for making as many trips back to the plazas.

Just when I run out of things to look at to distract myself from worrying about Orville's safety, he comes around from the shelter making his way back to the van.

"It looks pretty safe," says Orville after he swings open Marc's door. "They are pretty chill people if I am being honest."

"See? What did I tell you?" replies Marc, a smirk growing across his face.

"Oh be quiet! I don't need an 'I told you so' right now," chuckles Orville. "So, do you guys want to take a break here and ask these drifters if they have any ideas? It can't hurt to check.

"Anything to get me out of this car," I groan. "I'm getting restless sitting back here."

"Ah, getting tired of me, I see," jokes Ambrose. He makes a playful jab towards my ribs which I block with my hand.

Climbing out of the car and taking a few steps is a sweet relief for my cramped legs. Being out of the van provides me with a new perspective on the drifter community. I see there are more buildings than I estimated. There are likely close to thirty people who live here if not more. This must be what a more permanent drifter living arrangement looks like. It's nothing like I imagined yet it makes so much sense. Hopefully, someone here has some information.

"Welcome, everyone!" a tall, burly man exclaims. His windswept hair is tied back with a yellow bandana. I have never noticed before with the drifters but every person I can see in this settlement has some article of yellow on them. Maybe it's just this group but it still signifies them as a community.

"This is Enzo Dawson, the chief of this drifter clan," says Orville. We remain cautious of this situation but Orville greets the man with a handshake. "Enzo, this is Marc, Ambrose, and Luca."

"Pleasure to meet you all." Enzo's gaze fixes on me as if I'm a suspect in a crime. It's unnerving how he seems to peer through my skin, examining every secret I have ever held. "Tell me, Luca, what is your last name?"

"Um, it's Juniper. From my mother." He only asked my name but my nerves are skyrocketing.

"Hm...very well. Let's go grab some lunch."

"Oh, please! I am starving from driving all morning," says Ambrose. He is unfazed by Enzo, though, he is clearly good at hiding things from me. It's becoming hard for me to trust him given he and Violet kept being in a secret organization with my grandmother from me for years.

Enzo leads us into the marketplace in the center of the

settlement. Most stalls sell wares to patch up tents or fix seals in water canisters. There are seven stalls in total. Two stalls are selling food. Ambrose is already drooling at the food while I stand next to him with a knot in my stomach. One stall has fried okra, zucchini, and some other vegetables I don't recognize. I doubt they are grown out here in Yellow so they must be a shipment from Green. The other stall is selling roasted duck.

I can't even remember the last time I had meat. We aren't necessarily vegans in the Oasis, but there are not many animals here, especially on a commercial ranching level. If there is meat available, it is likely lab-grown and, frankly, not the best tasting.

"Eat what you please. It's on me," says Enzo.

"In that case, I'll take one of everything!" Ambrose replies. He has such ease when it comes to being comfortable around new people. "Luca, are you going to eat?"

"No, I'm fine. Eat for me," I try to joke but it comes out strained. I can see it dampens Ambrose's excitement, but I am not hungry.

After everyone else grabs some food, Enzo leads us into one of the larger huts just off the marketplace. The interior resembles a meeting hall with a large wood table at the front of the room and three chairs behind it. Facing the table are rows of skinny benches just wide enough to sit down. Comfortable? No, but they are practical. Everything in this room was made to be effortless to pack up and move with ease should the need arise.

"I'm really glad you all came," says Enzo as he takes a seat at the front table. I grab a spot on the second bench closest to him. An optimistic yet calculated approach. "To be honest, the drifters thought there would be more people wandering the desert after what transpired in the Oasis."

"So you expected us?" asks Marc.

"Assumed rather than expected, young man. We *assumed* there would be a distaste for Chu's leadership style that would send others on a search for answers. With the Oasis destroyed and controlled by a third party, where else would people turn? The answer, of course, is that it would be Yellow."

"Did you know about the attack? Were you an accomplice in all this?!" questions Orville with rising suspicion.

"No, no," asserts Enzo calmly. "We knew just as much as the rest of the Oasis. That day was a celebration with no widespread reason to attack anyone. The drifters were just as confused as I am sure you all were that day. I am saddened at the loss the Oasis felt that day and every day since."

"Things still aren't quite adding up..." says Orville.

"As drifters, we don't expect anything. Not our next meal, shower, or call to a loved one. We definitely didn't expect Lumos to ransack the entire Oasis. We may disagree, Orville, on the complexities of our scientific society, but no drifter played a part in bringing down the Machine. That I can assure you."

"Why exactly do you live all the way out here? Doesn't it get lonely?" I ask Enzo. I have only heard other's opinions of the drifters and am genuinely curious as to why they live as they do.

"Luca, wasn't it? Well, it isn't that we disagreed with having an AI, such as the Machine, in charge of the Oasis. We saw great promise in him and would have followed his leadership. However, the potential to exploit the technology was too high. We feared what we are seeing today: a return to old ways of governing, power trips, and chaos. The mission of the drifters was not to flee society but to evolve it. We are a broad, interconnected community of nomads. With no central figure in charge, each clan, in a sense, governs itself. But each individual is his own leader and in charge of his own destiny."

"Is that efficient?" I ask.

"I think that efficiency is not the key, Luca. Efficiency breeds competition, not cooperation. Cooperation and peace are the paths toward a simpler future. A future that won't repeat the ills of the past."

"Did you know my mother?" The question catches everyone off guard, even me. It had been sitting at the back of my mind since we got here. I want to save the Machine, but I also want to learn more about my mother.

"Unfortunately, I am afraid I do not. What was her name?"

"Never mind my asking," I brush off his question.

Embarrassed that I even asked. "Do you know where the Machine is?"

"You think he is still alive?"

"He has to be!" My hands clench into fists. "We were sent out here because we believe there is still hope. Without the Machine, we lose. With him by our side, we can take down Lumos and revive the Oasis."

"Spoken like a true warrior. There is always hope. But you have to fight for it. It won't come easy."

"I am prepared for it to be hard."

"Very well," Enzo measures me with a cold stare. "We assume you think the Machine is in Yellow if you have searched this far out for so long."

"It's the most logical."

"Will logic help you today or is introspection the winner?"

"How can I be introspective about this? It isn't about me."

"Ah, the key to understanding the drifters is countering your own thoughts. Everything is simultaneously about you and about everything but you. Tug on one thing and find it tied to everything else in the world."

"That still doesn't answer my question though. Do you know if the Machine is in Yellow or not?"

"Persistent," Enzo chuckles. "Yes, the Machine is likely hiding in Yellow. Lumos is too heavily guarding the central Oasis for him to operate there with how weak they made him.

He needs time to recuperate. I don't know where *exactly*, but if you have made it this far, you're bound to find him soon. Ross Ingrim was a tricky man, so I am sure the Machine is well hidden. Use every tree as a clue."

"Ok." I feel defeated. I can't even process what Enzo is saying anymore. The drifters don't know where the Machine is either. They were our last hope. They know the desert better than anyone.

"It's getting late. Should we start to head back?" I hear Ambrose ask Orville.

"Yeah, let's get going. Enzo, thank you for speaking with us," says Orville, extending his hand for a handshake.

"Anytime, good sir! You and your crew are always welcome here."

Everyone gets up to leave. I linger on the bench for just a moment longer, which feels like an eternity. The weight on my shoulders has grown even heavier after today's events.

"Luca," Enzo catches my attention as I head toward the exit. "I look forward to seeing you soon."

—

I find myself lying on my back on top of a soft, fuzzy blanket. Sunlight filters through a canopy of leaves towering above me. The peculiar thing is I don't remember where I am. I also can't move. Well, to be more accurate, I can't sit up. I feel my arms wave and my feet kick around me, yet my efforts to rise are in vain.

I tilt my head away from the sky toward the cool ground beneath me. The blanket I am lying on is a pale purple. That was my mother's favorite color, so this must be hers. There is not much to see in my vicinity. The thicket of flora growing underneath the canopy is perfectly balanced. Not too compact. Not too sparse. Precisely in between. Almost deliberate.

When I turn my head in the opposite direction, I notice an open door wedged into the hillside. I am unsure what awaits me inside, but I can't believe it is anything dangerous given the serenity of this place. I let my eyes slowly drift back to the canopy before closing them.

A short, heavy clank alerts me again to the open door on the hillside. Rather than being an empty doorway, a young woman stands just beyond the frame looking down at a tablet. After a few seconds, she lays the tablet on the ground by the door and strolls over to me. As her face comes into view, her details look familiar but wrong. I become even more confused when she bends down to pick me up. What am I? Where am I? Who is this?

"Luca," says the woman. She knows me. "One day, you'll come back to this place. I hope you treasure it as I treasure you."

This woman…I recognize her. She is my mother. But that

makes me too young to remember any of this.

"Luca!" my mother screams, but it is not her voice now. "Luca, wake up! We need to get out of the van."

My eyes flash open in panic. Ambrose stares back at me. He does not seem entirely panicked, though, I can tell something has gone wrong. I scramble out of the car, attempting to shake off my strange dream. *Why was I a baby?*

Marc is ushering us out and away from the van. It takes a solid minute before I grasp the situation. We are stopped because the front of the van is on fire.

"How did this happen?" Marc says worriedly. "Everything was working fine until we crossed the bridge coming out of Yellow."

"What if it was sabotage?" questions Orville. "I told you those drifters were up to no good."

"Maybe you're right…"

"Guys! I don't think anybody sabotaged our van in that camp," I interject. "The drifters have no reason to hurt us. If they were going to attack us, why would they stop us here? And if it was someone other than the drifters, say Lumos, then we are also in the clear because they don't know we came out here. So let's just calm down and figure out how we are going to get home."

"Agreed. This is *totally* normal for vans to do. Mine just burst into flames last week!" jokes Ambrose. While he eased some tension, his humor doesn't solve our predicament.

"We are in Orange. Does anyone have a signal yet?" I ask.

Chapter 4

Getting back to Blue is going to be technically challenging, to say the least. The van is pretty much totaled after the engine burst into flames. Orville and Marc managed to put the fire out but, at that point, it was too late. The belts are melted off, the wiring is in disarray, and the engine block has seen better days. The peculiar thing is that Orville and Marc can't find the ignition source for the fire. It looks to be spontaneous. If I take the fire as a sign, it doesn't bode well for our mission. We won't be able to find the Machine if we get stranded in the middle of nowhere.

We are also in a communication dead zone where we broke down. Communication has been spotty ever since Chu and Lumos took over the Oasis. With the Machine, we had signal everywhere except in the farthest reaches of Yellow. The rest of the districts never experienced a blackout with the Machine. Lumos, however, destroyed much of the communications equipment in their attack and subsequent search for the Machine. Their tactics have completely cut off portions of the Oasis from each other. This complicates our mission as it makes it challenging to communicate with my grandmother and the rest of the team back home.

Only Ambrose, Orville, Marc, and I came out to Yellow to search for the Machine here. Violet and Jasmine stayed back in Blue to work on a separate mission. I can only imagine the struggles they are facing with being so intimate with Lumos's operation. If they get caught, it could spell doom for the entire team. So far, we are working in secret. Lumos knows that my friends and I are resisting their tyranny, but they don't know the degree to which our network reaches. Even I don't know the full extent. Helen keeps a tight ship.

We abandoned the van and walked about a mile deeper into Orange before any of us received a signal. We must have been too close to Yellow when we broke down. I don't think we had a signal the entire time we were out in Yellow. It makes for a lonely experience, especially, when we are used to being so connected to each other, but it also makes it much easier to conceal our movements from Lumos.

Currently, I have made myself comfortable on a post

jutting out of the ground at an angle. We aren't far from the RAMON station now so we could walk there. However, we likely won't catch a ride. Lumos has repaired some of the track but, in general, RAMON continues to remain out of commission since the attack. The same goes for the O.A.I.T.s. They are just hunks of junk now. Without the Machine, they aren't connected to anything nor do they have any information, which defeats their entire purpose. Lumos also hasn't rebuilt the Tree, the symbol of the Oasis. A symbol of our future living synergistically with nature. The sky feels empty without it.

Given all this, our only option for getting back to Blue quickly is waiting for a ride. Angelica left Blue a while ago, so she should be here soon. Yet it feels as if time has stopped and she is never going to reach us. Every time I feel my mood improving, dread sneaks right back in full force.

Just when I think all is lost, Angelica pulls up in her blue car. Unfortunately, the team's only large vehicle is now a melted mess in Yellow. We are going to be cramped. Since Orville is the tallest among the four of us, we let him have the front seat while Marc, Ambrose, and I cram into the rear seats. It is a tight fit but there is surprisingly more room than I expected.

I worry that the ride back is going to drag on but I feel myself getting sleepy almost immediately after Angelica starts driving. The quiet hum of the electric engine, combined with being fatigued from a long day of meeting people and having our car break down, makes my eyes heavy. I lean my head against Ambrose's shoulder and he lays his head on mine. It's a simple, comforting embrace that makes me feel safe. I let my eyes shut close.

In a moment, I feel the car come to a stop. I open my eyes and lift my head from Ambrose's shoulder. To my surprise, I see my house. Clearly, I fell asleep and lost track of time. After being gone from home for so long, seeing my house causes a rush of emotions to flow through my body. Tears threaten to fall down my cheeks but I hold them back, embracing the emotions and letting them pass.

Stretching my legs after getting out of the car feels wonderful. I look up to the front door and see Helen and Violet standing there. I have so much to tell them, but at the same time, it doesn't seem like we learned anything new. Maybe they can decipher what Enzo said.

"Welcome home, Luca," Violet greets me with a grin. "We are excited you're back."

"Thanks, Violet. It's good to see you, too." As I approach the door, they embrace me in a hug. My tired body sinks into their arms. "It's too late. I need a nap."

"Don't let him kid you," says Ambrose. "Slept the whole way home. He was out within a mile of where Angelica picked us up."

"Not even true," I respond.

"Plus he snored the whole time!" adds Marc.

"Everyone let's get inside," says Helen. "We have important things to discuss."

"Gigi, can't this wait until morning?" I plead. The comfort of a real bed is calling my name. Sleeping in a car doesn't match the coziness of the covers.

"No," says Helen, who turns to walk inside without allowing time for an argument. "I'm still waiting on a couple of people, but everyone else is here now. I just need to grab something from my office."

"Want us to head down or wait for you and the others?" asks Violet. They seem to have become Helen's right-hand person since we left for the desert. I'm glad. Violet has proven they are fit for the job.

"Go ahead. I'll bring the others when they arrive."

I realize I am still leaning into Violet's embrace. I wonder why they haven't pushed me away yet.

"Oh, Violet, won't you please carry us down?" says Ambrose, embracing both of us.

"Boys, this is serious," says Violet in a stern voice. They push both of us off with that remark. Violet means business, too.

I know we are in serious times, but even I'm not devoid of having a little fun to break up the monotony. Something seems to have changed between Violet and my grandmother since Ambrose and I have been gone. The two of them have grown closer, though, I wasn't aware of the true extent of their relationship before the attack. Perhaps I will never understand it.

The ride down the elevator in the garden shed is eerily quiet. The only sounds I can hear are the hum of the lift system and everyone's breathing. Being in such close quarters makes even the faintest breath particularly noticeable.

When the doors open, I see there are a few people inside. I can't tell if it's because I just don't remember them or if it's been too long since I've seen these people, but I'm struggling to recall their names. They seem just as downtrodden as I feel. The vibe of this place has gone downhill since we left. Everyone was so hopeful six months ago. Now, it feels more hopeless.

"Willow, can you please start the holo map?" asks Violet. I remember who they are talking with now. Willow Omongo is just slightly younger than my mother would have been. She is a teacher at a nearby elementary school. She was never around me much, although, I do know her child. He is about twelve years old. I don't see him around, so Willow's involvement is either held secret from her family or they are just at home sleeping. Both seem reasonable.

"Absolutely, Violet. Is Helen not coming?" Willow replies.

"She just needed to grab something from inside the house. She will be down shortly."

"Men, it's nice to see you back from the desert," says Willow, turning her attention to Ambrose, Orville, Marc, and me. "I hope you found us some information."

"I'm afraid we didn't make much progress with the drifters," replies Orville. Whatever hope was left in the room disappears with that comment.

"We did get a clue from Enzo Dawson," I say. "He is in the clan leadership at the settlement we stopped at last. I think he gave me a clue but I don't understand what he was trying to say."

"Yes, I've met Enzo before," says Willow. I'm shocked she knows who I am talking about. I didn't expect anyone to know specific drifters. "He is a good man, with a strong commitment to his people and his word. But he can be difficult. I assume any clue from him will require some deciphering."

"I just worry we don't have time to decipher his cryptic messages."

I hear the hum of the shed lift again. Helen must be coming down with the others.

"Turn on the television!" shouts Helen as soon as the door opens. "Chu is making an announcement."

"I'm on it," announces Violet as they make strides to the left side of the room to power on the television. "What's going on?"

"I don't know, but it can't be anything good."

"…to you live from Monument Square, this is Monica Small," the news report had just started as Violet turned on the television. "Tonight may be gloomy but brighter days are on the horizon. In just a few moments, Commander Balo Chu will take the stage to announce an update on the situation regarding the radicals who attacked the Oasis six months ago. We know everyone at home is looking for answers and tonight may just be the night. Everyone, it's Commander Chu coming out on stage now."

The camera pans out from the reporter, revealing a crowd gathered in front of the amphitheater stage. It's odd seeing so many people there considering how late it is. I assumed most would be asleep by now. I know I am ready for bed.

"This has to be staged, doesn't it?" Ambrose mutters beside me. "Like c'mon, there's no way people are *that* excited to hear Chu speak at this hour."

"At least he hasn't built statues of himself yet," I whisper under my breath.

"Hello, and thank you all for coming on such short notice, especially so late it is," says Chu. "it's for all of you that we have been working so tirelessly to bring justice back to the Oasis. Without your support, these rebels may have never been caught."

"Rebels?" I ask. "What group is he talking about?"

"He's the rebel leading Lumos! What is he even talking about?!" exclaims Ambrose.

"Quiet down you two," responds Helen biting the skin on her thumb anxiously. She is clearly as nervous as we are but doesn't want to show it.

"Last night, we apprehended five individuals snooping around both the command center and the Tree rubble. After just a brief interrogation, it became clear these five individuals were all connected and were planning another attack. Their stories didn't line up and actions speak louder than words. It was determined these five individuals are members of Lumos, or as you may know them, the group responsible for bringing the Oasis to its knees six months ago."

"He's separating himself from Lumos!" says Violet. "He's trying to make it seem like he's on the people's side."

They're right. That is definitely what is happening. I just don't know why he waited until now. There are so many questions running through my mind. Are these "rebels" even real? What happened to Lumos being the saviors of the Oasis?

"Tonight, we take back what was lost." Chu motions toward the other side of the stage and a team of Oasis Response cadets march out. Five blindfolded individuals, handcuffed and chained together with their hands behind their backs are dragged onto the platform. They are forced to kneel and their blindfolds are removed. "Tonight, we take back what was stolen from so many of us. These five rebels will pay for their crimes"

"They're just kids..." Helen whispers. She has tears rolling quietly down her cheek. Angelica stands to place a hand on Helen's shoulder. An embrace of solitude. Angelica is also fighting back tears. *What is happening?* There is something I don't understand about this situation.

"Do you know them, Gigi?" She only shakes her head no, her eyes are still glued to the scene unfolding on screen.

"Tonight," Chu declares coldly, "these five Lumos rebels will be executed."

"He can't do that!" Violet shoots to their feet.

My thoughts are racing. An execution in the Oasis? It's never happened. We don't even have weapons...guns. Just as I think there isn't a way someone could be so cruel, another cadet comes from off-stage with a case of five loaded pistols. One for each prisoner.

My brain is too groggy to compute what is happening. Why is Chu deciding to do this? What is his goal? Why did the older members of our group seem to know what was coming before he even said it? I've been looking away from the screen but turn back when Chu says two simple words: "Do it."

His voice cuts through the air like a blade and five shots ring out. The sound echoes across Monument Square. My stomach retches and I nearly vomit. Everyone is silent, frozen in fear as the five lifeless bodies are dragged off stage. A solid minute passes before Chu speaks again as if nothing happened.

"Well, now that we have that settled, we can address the other pressing matter of the night. In addition to Lumos, there is another group working to undermine the authority of my administration. A group that seeks to resurrect the dangerous entity known as the Machine. The entity that slaughtered the Legislative Council after the attack after being severely damaged by the collapse of the Tree. This group, under the command of Helen Juniper, is setting its eyes on a second societal overthrow after we have just found peace."

Gasps ripple throughout the room. Everyone in the room turns to look at my grandmother. We thought Lumos and Chu had no idea we were still operating. Now they are calling out Helen in one move.

"We are unsure of the size of this rebel organization. We only know it is run by Helen Juniper, the mother of the late Amelia Juniper. She is considered to be an at-large radical criminal. We need your help to identify her supporters and bring these rebels to justice."

"Thank you for tuning in, this was Monica Small, live from Monument Square. Back to you Jaymes." The broadcast ends. Helen remains frozen, her hand covering her mouth in disbelief.

"Everyone go home," she finally whispers after another moment of silence.

"But—" tries Angelica.

"I said go home. Be with your families. And conceal the fact that you have ever been here if you have any smarts about you."

Everyone besides Violet, Ambrose, and I slowly take the cue and head out of the bunker. Helen remains frozen in place. Her gaze remains fixed on the now blank screen.

"I meant everyone, you three. Go," Helen mumbles.

With that, Ambrose and Violet start toward the lift, but I stay frozen. My stomach churns and my mind reels from the executions. When he notices I am not following, Ambrose returns and grips my arm, alerting me to his presence and to the need to leave. I glance at my grandmother. I am torn between leaving her alone as she wishes or staying with her to be a comforting presence. I don't know if I'd be much help, though. I may just make matters worse in the state I am in.

The fresh, night air is brisk when we step out of the shed but it does little to soothe my nausea. Ambrose and Violet are talking about something but I am blocking them out. Even though I am now on solid ground, I feel like I am going to vomit. I sneak away from Ambrose and Violet over to the seating area next to the small koi pond my grandmother tends hoping the peaceful water calms my nerves. But nothing eases the knot of my guilt and anxiety.

"Hey, mind if I join you?" asks Ambrose. I glance up to see Violet walking away.

"Yeah," it's all I can make out. I feel more hopeless than everyone in that bunker combined. I have never witnessed someone executed on the news, let alone be shot, besides Samantha during the raid on Lumos.

"What's on your mind?" Ambrose asks gently.

"What isn't?" I'm silent for a bit before responding.

"Can you be more specific, please?"

"We just watched five innocent people get murdered on live TV. We spent weeks in the desert searching for some clue to find the Machine and got nowhere. Now, Chu is tightening his grip, and Lumos – or "not Lumos" – is right on our tails to officially overthrow the Oasis and create some wicked dystopian future. Is that specific enough for you, Ambrose?" I snap at the end.

"I'm just trying to help and I need to understand what you are thinking."

"Then maybe pay attention to what matters," I mutter angrily, instantly regretting it. I hope Ambrose didn't hear what I said.

"Excuse me?" Too late, he heard. "You don't think I pay attention?"

"Ahh, that's not the point."

"Then what is the point?"

"It just seems like sometimes you don't take anything seriously!"

"I thought you liked my joking?"

"I need you present in the moment right now. We are losing everything we used to know, and I'm not sure how much more of this I can take. I feel worthless, empty, and numb. The end feels so near it's terrifying, Ambrose. What if we can't save the Machine in time?"

I get up and start pacing around the pond, my anxiety rising with each step. I need to keep moving or I'm going to crawl out of my skin. I didn't notice at first, but Ambrose is taking a while to respond.

"Luca...I don't know what to say to you to keep you happy. The Machine, this group we made, it doesn't matter anymore. Maybe its time we let it go. It's over."

"Over?!" I stop pacing. My blood is suddenly boiling. "How can you say all of this is over? Do you just think that Chu is going to let you waltz back to the greenhouses and allow you to live out your life after what you just witnessed?"

"I—"

"I can't just move on!" I cut Ambrose off. "This entire thing has been and continues to be about my family's legacy. I would have been able to prepare much sooner, but the rest of you decided it best to keep everything a secret from me.

To operate right under my nose! I didn't even know who my own mother was. Then to come to find out, she created the Machine and the Oasis. All too late! Now it's my responsibility to find the Machine and bring him back, all the while having a murderous maniac running the Oasis and hunting us down."

"It wasn't my choice to hide this from you."

"I just want to know!" Ambrose reaches for me, but I step back. My vision is getting blurry from the tears welling in my eyes.

Silence falls between us. Neither of us knows what to say next.

"I think this has gone too far," I say, breaking the silence.

"What is that supposed to mean?"

"You know what it means, Ambrose. It's time for me to call this."

"Luca, please," Ambrose stands and approaches me.

I take a step back as he gets close. Tears start to flow down my cheeks. I don't want to, but I know what needs to happen.

"Ambrose, I love you, but it's time. Too much has happened. I can't be your boyfriend anymore."

Ambrose reaches out for my hand again, but I turn and head inside my backdoor. Part of me hopes I'm doing this to keep him safe. The other part knows that I can't handle this relationship anymore and breaking up is really to keep me safe. Either way, I need to focus on protecting my grandmother and saving the Machine.

Chapter 5

"Why did you send everyone away last night?" I ask my grandmother as she hands me a bowl of cereal.

"It was for the best, Luca. You and I both know that."

"So it's just us now? What are we going to do?"

"What exactly did Enzo Dawson tell you out in the desert?" Helen sits down, her expression turns even more serious.

"It didn't make any sense," I hesitate. "I don't know what to make of it."

"What did he say, Luca?" Her eyes narrow slightly.

"Let's see," I sigh. "He told me to be introspective, to not rely on logic, and then 'use every tree as a clue.'"

She nods slowly, a faint smile tugging at her lips. "Ah, Enzo. Still as tricky as ever."

"You knew him, too?" I say with surprise. "Willow knew him, as well."

"I mostly know of him. We were acquaintances at best. He was good friends with Ross Ingrim, so what he said doesn't sound out of place."

"So...does his clue make sense to you?"

"Well, not exactly. Perhaps he was being literal about the trees. Maybe we should start there. When you were in Yellow, did you come across any trees?"

"Gigi, I promise you the only trees in Yellow are the ones in my dreams," I shake my head.

"Did your dreams of the trees provide any clues?"

"I mean, I haven't thought much about it," I admit. "I seemed to be a baby in the dream. I couldn't move around much. But even if the dream did provide a clue, how would Enzo know about it?"

"Maybe he was just guessing?" She muses.

"He did love to say the drifters only assume. But are there even trees clear out in Yellow? We looked everywhere and never saw a single one."

Suddenly we hear a knocking at the front door making us both freeze in fear. Panic flashes through me. I can't help but think it could be Chu here to take Helen away. After a few moments, we both slide our chairs back. Our movements are synchronized by fear. Together, we approach the door.

38

My hands are trembling as I reach for the handle. The cold metal knob sends chills through my fingertips as I twist it open. Standing on the stoop is a face I am not expecting. To my shock, Violet is standing on the stoop, looking as bold and empowered as ever. They've got something planned. I'm too stunned to say anything, so I peer behind them instead. Jasmine, Orville, and Marc are perched at the bottom step looking at me intensely for a response.

"I…I…what are you doing here?" It's all I can manage to muster. They aren't even supposed to be here. It's too dangerous for them to be around Helen and me.

"We know we were told to leave and forget all about our mission to save the Oasis. But frankly, home is kinda boring. And besides, we agreed we simply can't forget about our mission."

"But Violet—"

"No buts about it, Luca." Their voice is firm and unyielding. "We know the risks and we have accepted that. You don't get to tell us no, m'kay?"

"Luca, who's at the door?" Helen calls from the table. I hear her footsteps approaching the door.

"Hi, Helen!" the group chimes in unison.

"Oh my!" Helen's face lights up in surprise. "Hurry, come inside."

"So we've discussed it and we think that heading back out

to Yellow with a fresh pair of eyes is a good idea. Take one last look around the district just in case we missed something," says Violet.

"Yeah, there's gotta be something else. We can't give up," adds Jasmine. "Violet and I spent a lot of time researching Chu's movements and actions regarding the Machine. He has no clue where the Machine could be, so we are safe returning to Yellow."

"And there could be a clue," I say as I glance toward Helen looking for approval. She nods, so I continue. "Enzo Dawson told me to 'look in every tree.' At first, I thought he was crazy, but now I can't rule anything out."

"Exactly!" exclaims Violet. "Trees in Yellow. Peculiar but not impossible."

"When should we head back out?" asks Marc.

"You should all leave now," says Helen stepping forward. "No time to waste." She's practically shoving us out the door already.

"Hold on, are you not coming?" I question. Helen shakes her head.

"No. It's best if I stay here. Someone needs to stay behind and gather intel. I'll handle that. You go find the Machine, but go get changed first."

I run up the stairs in a flash. I grab a pair of pants and a shirt from the floor and the jacket Ambrose gave me from the hook on the back of the door. As I rush back downstairs, I can't help but think that I probably didn't need to bring this jacket. We aren't together anymore, but it's too late to change my mind. Everyone is waiting for me.

"Gigi, please be safe," I say. I give her the biggest hug I can muster. I don't like her staying here alone but she's adamant about staying behind.

"You be safe out there," she whispers in my ear. I don't want to let go, but eventually, Helen pulls away from my grasp. I know it's time to go.

"Have you spoken with Ambrose today?" Violet asks me as we walk to the car.

"No," I say curtly. I'm unwilling to elaborate.

The car is warm from the sun when we climb in. I sit in the back with Violet and Jasmine, while Orville and Marc take the front. Luckily, this car has more room than Angelica's cramped one. The car spurs to life and the landscape outside blurs as we drive.

Time passes and my muscles ache from sitting too long. We just crossed back into Yellow a few miles ago, but it feels like we have been driving for days already. I forgot how much I disliked being in a car for this long. I hope we reach a stopping point soon. Every part of me aches to stretch out.

None of us know where to look for trees in the Yellow District. Not once have I seen a single tree in the handful of times I've been out here. Orville suspects we will need to venture further out than before. Last time, we searched the sections of Yellow closest to the rest of the Oasis. Places that also seem likely to support trees. But Enzo told me to abandon logic and trust instinct. So I am doing just that and agree with Orville's plan.

We have passed the final solar array and are reaching the boundaries of the Oasis itself. After this point, it *should* just be a wasteland. Yet, everything is adding up to mean the opposite. Could the world out here instead hold a forest?

I am getting tired. Orville must be, too, because he stops the car and switches spots with Marc who is groggy but rested from the nap he took on the way out here. Once we start moving again, I slide down in my seat so I can rest my head more comfortably. I'm fighting the urge to sleep, but we don't know how much longer we will be on the road.

I turn my head to look out the window. My eyes are growing heavier with every passing mile. The sun's heat casts a shimmering mirage on the ground, luring me into a slumber. The warmth of the sun feels comforting, a feeling I have been lacking these past months. It's not the answer I am looking for, but it's better than the emptiness gnawing at me. My eyes finally close and I think I have lost my fight with sleep. But before I drift off completely, sirens blare in my head. I jolt awake, certain I saw something. But where did it go? I sit up straight and brush off the sleepiness. Peering out the window, I don't see much of anything. There's only the endless stretch of dust and barren horizon. Perhaps I am just seeing things that don't exist.

I scan the horizon again, squinting hard trying to see. Maybe it's just a trick of the heat. But then I see something. I think I saw a dark cluster off in the distance. I try to follow it through the haze, but we hit a dusty patch causing the car to kick up dirt making it difficult to see. I keep looking through the gaps in the dust hoping whatever it was comes back into view.

It's faint — barely visible through the dust — but it's there. Trees. I know it. Just barely visible on the horizon.

"Marc, take a left. We need to go this way."

"Okay, but what exactly am I headed for?" replies Marc.

"Straight ahead. Do you see that dark clump that stands out from the dirt?"

"What do you think it is?"

"Trees. It has to be trees."

"There's nothing out here, though. What makes you think there is a random clump of trees on those hills?"

"It just feels right. It's not logical, but logic isn't going to help us anyway."

Violet, Jasmine, and Orville are all awake again and are staring off into the distance trying to make sense of what I see. I am not sure if I am making this all up, officially losing my mind, or seeing trees, but I can't give up hope. Not when it's all I have left to hope for.

"Maybe. I still can't tell," says Jasmine. The terrain is getting hillier so even I lose what we are trying to see when we go down the backside of a hill.

"Just wait," I plead. I'm urging my friends to hold out and trust me. We are heading up this long, steep hill. Once we are on top, we should be close enough to see the cluster better.

But as we crest the hill, all that stands ahead of us is dry, barren hills.

"I'm sorry, guys," I mutter. "I was wrong."

"No, I don't think so!" says Violet. "Marc, keep driving up this next hill and angle left."

"Sure can do, Violet."

As we climb the next hill and angle our direction to the north, I see it. Green! It's a small forest nestled in the valley below. We just weren't high enough to see it. The trees were in a low section but must have reflected in the heat mirage somehow. Or maybe I just made an extremely lucky guess as to where they were since no one else saw them.

"Yes!" I shout, and excitement floods through me. "Head that way."

As we descend, the cluster of trees comes fully into view. It's not a large cluster – maybe only a few acres big. The small forest nestles right up into the base of another large hill to the east, but it stands out like an oasis in the wasteland. I'm assuming there is a small spring in the middle of the forest because there are no other reasons for there to be all this foliage out here.

"We are about ten miles outside the southern boundary of the Oasis," says Marc. "No wonder we never saw this before."

"I still can't believe this exists outside of Yellow," adds Orville.

"There are people there," Jasmine says suddenly. "Near the trees."

"I see them, too," says Violet. "But who are they?"

"Drifters," I sigh with a hint of disdain.

We reach the bottom of the hill and I notice the drifters standing by the trees are holding stun rifles. Peculiar as I never saw a stun rifle anywhere in the settlement we visited. As Marc parks the car, the two men start walking toward us. I'm ready to get out of this car so I take the initiative and get out first.

I move to the front of the car, studying the drifter's faces trying to gauge if they are hostile. That's when I notice a third figure hiding in the shadows of the trees. As the sunlight hits him, my breath catches and I instantly recognize him. It's Enzo Dawson.

"Ah, so you figured out the clues I gave you," shouts Enzo from afar. A sly grin spreads across his face. "We were hoping you'd find your way here."

"So you knew exactly where this place was when we met you before, didn't you?" I respond. My frustration is boiling over. "You made me go through all that just to end up here?"

"Correct," Enzo replies smoothly. He and the other two men stop a few feet from the car. My friends have all joined me outside the car now, too. "Every drifter knows of this place. But we had to make sure you were who you claimed to be. That you weren't Lumos agents coming to destroy the Machine."

"So he's alive!" My anger vanishes in an instant and is replaced by a surge of hope. I am barely able to contain my relief.

"Well, he is, but he's not in the best of shape, unfortunately. We need your help."

Chapter 6

"This place has been a source of life for our people since we first came to the Oasis," says Enzo who is leading us deeper into the thick tangle of trees. "We helped the founders conceal it from the rest of the Oasis."

"Did you lie about knowing my mother?" I ask, struggling to keep up with his long strides.

"You shall learn many things, Luca. But, yes, I knew your mother very well. Amelia had a brilliant mind."

"Why didn't you tell me you knew her?"

"Because I simply wasn't sure you were who you claimed to be. Many knew Amelia and what she created. Some adored her, while others...not so much. When you showed up after all this time looking for answers about the Machine, I couldn't just take your word at face value. No one else can know about this place, so I had to test you first."

"Wait, you knew me when I was little?"

"Amelia often brought a certain young boy named Luca here. It was a difficult journey to make alone with a baby, but your mother was a tough person who did what she wanted, regardless of difficulty. It was over fifteen years ago since I last saw you, though."

"Do you know what happened to her?" My voice tightens, bracing for a truth I might not want to hear.

"No. One day she just never showed back up and we lost all contact. Communicating with her was sporadic and the system was only in place in case she had an emergency. When months passed and she didn't return, we feared the worst. We knew Lumos must still be active, so we have protected this place since ever since."

"Where are we going?" We have been following a small footpath through the trees and I see a clearing up ahead.

"There's a spring in this clearing that feeds this whole area," Enzo explains. "It's the only spot with water and flora this far out. And there's something I need to show you."

When we break into the clearing, I stop dead in my tracks. This place is so familiar. It's only a moment before I realize it is the same clearing from my dream. No, not a dream. It must have been a memory. There's a large pool of water where the spring bubbles to the surface, spreading moisture into the mossy ground. Everything here is alive and vibrant. It's completely different from the desert beyond the trees.

Then I see it. A door pressed into the hill. The same door I dreamed my mother coming out of. Only it is obscured by tangled vines hanging from the tree above now.

I approach the door and brush the vines aside. A small, dusty control panel is embedded into the hillside. There are a few fingerprint spots in the dust where someone recently opened it.

"Go ahead," Enzo says, standing behind me. "The door is unlocked."

"What is this place?" I mumble.

"When the Machine turned on here, we didn't know what to do. So we left him in peace hoping an acolyte or Amelia would return. But I think he is lost. Maybe you are the key, Luca."

"Me? What makes you think I will know what to do," I say as I push the door open and enter into a small room. Dust coats everything inside - a couch, old bookshelves, and a desk with a flickering computer monitor. There's a small, compact server sitting next to the desk. I walk closer to the computer monitor because there is some video playing that I can barely make out through the dust.

"He has just been watching this since the computer turned

on," Enzo says.

I wipe away the dust. My breath catches in my throat when I see what's playing. I immediately recognize who is in the video. My mom is standing up on a rock looking out at the distant dunes. The camera is shaky but I can make out the once-great sand dunes. We still have the dunes in the Oasis today, but the winds changed during Calamity so they are not as big as they once were.

"Oh, isn't this place lovely?" Amelia's voice echoes through time.

"I thought you'd like it," a man's voice responds shakily but warmly. "I can't believe you never came here before Calamity. It used to be even more beautiful."

"We'll make it beautiful again," Amelia lifts her binoculars and searches the horizon.

The camera holds steady and a man walks into view. It must be on a tripod now. Though I've only seen pictures, I can tell the man is Ross Ingrim. As Ross walks closer to my mom, she turns around and embraces him in a hug.

Why is this video playing? I wonder. My heart is racing.

Then the video flickers with static, cutting to another scene. Ross must have had a retro film camera he used to record. This time my mom is filming. She turns the camera around to face herself as Ross watches men unload a semi-truck full of large crates marked "fragile electronics." It must be the Machine's servers.

The video goes static again. Now, my mom is sitting on the floor. Behind her are large windows that reveal the distinctive buildings of the Oasis. My mom and Ross accomplished their dream. But there are two differences. One, my mom is pregnant. I know it's with me because there is a calendar above the desk off to the side of the room. The date is November 17, 2032. Four months before my birthday. The other difference is that Ross is using a cane when he comes into the frame. He looks sick. I can't make out what they are saying.

The video cuts out again and a fourth begins to play. This time, my mom is cradling me. I don't look to be very old. She's crying and hasn't said anything. She stares into the camera, her sorrow is overwhelming. The pain behind her eyes is making me tear up, as well.

"This video," Amelia finally says. She is addressing baby me. "This video will likely be my last one. It was something we did together. But I want you, my son, to know this."

Her words are soft and full of grief. "Ross is dead. The Oasis assumed it was coming because he had been in hiding for six months. Ross didn't want people to see his weakness. The cancer…took over quickly. There was nothing we could do. He died a few weeks after you were born." There's another pause filled with her sobbing. I feel a tightness in my chest as I watch her break down.

"I just don't know what to do now." The defeat in her voice puts a pit in my stomach.

The video dissolves into more static, but this time it goes back to the beginning and starts replaying the videos. I start clicking around trying to figure out why the videos are repeating, or at least to understand why they are playing in the first place. When I hover the mouse over the close button, a message appears on the screen: *Please don't turn them off.*

I freeze and my heart skips a beat. It's the Machine. He's watching these videos – clinging to them - because it's all he has of his family, of his past, of a time long gone. It's all he has left. No Oasis. No people. He barely has any memories now. There isn't much computer hardware in this room. *How is the Machine even operating?*

Tears well up in my eyes and I can't hold back anymore. The Machine is so vulnerable right now and is so close to slipping away forever. If I lose him, I'll be losing the only connection I have to the family I never got to know. It will feel like losing them all over again. My family is in these videos. I lost control, too, and reacted when I fought with Ambrose. At that moment, I lost my future, and now I feel so overwhelmed. I'm lost...just like my mom was.

"Don't worry," I say through the tears. "It's me, Luca. I'm here to help."

Chapter 7

Violet and Jasmine grab my shoulders sensing I'm not in the best place. I'm thankful for them. Their presence is grounding and pulls me away from the overwhelming weight of my emotions. I wipe away my tears, steadying myself.

"I need to fix the corrupted file Lumos placed in the Machine's code," I say, trying to focus through my swirling thoughts.

"What can we do to help?" Violet asks with a steady tone.

"I'm gonna need a way to communicate with the Machine after we leave. Communication may not be fully operational by the time we leave, but we need to let the drifters know what to do next. We can't leave him here alone. See if there is a transmitter in this room."

"On it," Violet nods. They immediately start rummaging through boxes while I sit down and open my laptop. My mind races with possibilities, but none of them seem good enough. I must figure out how to fix his code. If I can't do that, there is no chance of returning the Machine to the Oasis. I recognize the repeating pattern in the Machine's code I saw on the O.A.I.T. months ago. That single repeating line...I had thought it could be a constraint or a ping. I also thought it was the Machine writing it. Now I know that it is a constraint. A single corrupted file lodged deep within the Machine's code, spreading through the system like a virus and keeping the Machine from fixing himself. If I can patch the source, it should fix everything.

What to do? My foot is tapping rapidly and my fingers are fidgety. I rub my leg trying to get the anxious nerves out. Then, I feel something in my pocket. It's the thumb drive my grandmother gave me. I know what it's designed to do as I looked more into it since she gave it to me. Using the thumb drive will be a quick and effective way of removing all of the code Lumos injected into the Machine when he was vulnerable. However, in doing so, the Machine would lose every one of his memories. Memories of building the Oasis. Of Amelia and Ross. I would kill him with this thumb drive.

NO! There's got to be another way. Just get out of your head and think!

I pull out the thumb drive, turning it over in my hand.

Maybe I don't use the thumb drive how it is intended. "Throw logic out the window, right?" I glance over at Enzo standing in the doorway.

"Exactly. Never take anything for granted." Enzo smiles faintly.

Taking a deep breath, I plug the thumb drive into my laptop. I disabled the Wifi and Bluetooth a while ago, so there is no way for the Machine to accidentally connect to the laptop while I am working on this fix. This is risky, though. If I do it wrong, I could kill the Machine.

You can't think like this. Your mom was the Creator of the Machine, she must have instilled some of her knowledge within you.

My hands shake as the program from the thumb drive starts running. The code is brutal. I see the destruction it would cause if I plugged it into the server that the Machine is on. The program's goal is to tear the Machine to pieces, expose all the hidden bits of code, and then place him back together in the most basic way possible. I'm glad I didn't plug this drive into the computer the Machine is on. There was no start button and it would have left the Machine unrecognizable.

I can construct a patch for the Machine using the code from this drive now that I have it running. It'll work like a bandage, masking the effects of the virus allowing the Machine to operate normally. At least, as normal as I can muster in this situation.

"Violet, have you found anything useful in those boxes?"

"We've got one more box to go through, but no transmitters yet."

It won't take me long to finish this patch. I am not a professional coder, but I know my way around a computer system. And I know the Machine's code better than most. After all, I was obsessed with learning all about him. I know his code. I just need to be confident in what I am making.

I'm confident the patch will work. I've been able to study the problem and analyze it thoroughly, and the thumb drive gave me what I needed to create it. But I am in my head and my hands are shaking as I insert another thumb drive into the laptop to copy the patch.

"Did you figure something out?" asks Jasmine.

"I hope so," I say at first. "No, I know it will work. It has too."

I pull the thumb drive from the laptop. My hands are trembling so badly right now that my body is practically quaking. I can't hold them steady. If Ambrose were here, he'd know how to comfort my nerves. If only I acted more reasonably. We are all under so much stress.

I use the computer to stabilize my hand as I insert the drive. I didn't program a start button either. The patch starts running as soon as it connects.

"Now all that's left is to wait," I mutter, trying to steady my voice.

"We found something," Violet says, rushing over with an old device. "This should work for long-range communication."

"Thanks, I'll plug it in now so he can reach us when he is ready."

The Machine seems less confused already. I notice the videos stop playing in the background, but he is still quiet. He's more quiet and less helpful than he was back at the bunker in Purple. Rather, all that has happened since I plugged in the patch is a message that popped up. It reads: *Thank you, Luca.* I swallow the lump in my throat. The fight to save the Machine isn't over. It's going to take even more than this patch to save the Oasis. But we are on a path now.

"Will you help us?" I turn to Enzo. My voice is quiet but firm. For the first time, he looks worried. It's an emotion I have not seen him carry. "Help us to save the Oasis and bring back the Machine?"

"I'm afraid we can't interfere," he says shaking his head. "We have done what we can to protect him."

"Please…" My voice cracks. I am practically begging Enzo. "We can't do this alone." Marc and Orville step into the room and I can tell they sense the desperation in my voice.

Our numbers are too small to fight against Lumos and Chu's Oasis Response. Chu has them under his grip. The whole Oasis really. The people are so scared they don't realize the person leading them is the one they should fear the most. We need the drifters' help. If they are my mother's secret protectors of the Machine, they must be able to intervene. If we don't win, the Oasis and the Machine will be lost forever.

"It's getting dark, we should go," announces Orville which interrupts the heavy silence.

Violet comes to grab my hand to lead me out of the room. She is going to have to drag me out. I feel numb and disconnected from everything again. It's not fear, sadness, or regret. I just feel…nothing. I don't know what I am supposed to feel anymore.

Walking back through the meadow, I am reminded of my dream. I wish I could return to that time. To be young and carefree, living life beneath a canopy of hope and love. A simple life full of family. But that's gone now.

Stepping out of the small forest and back into the desert, I am reminded of the harsh reality of my world. I have nothing left but my grandmother and a weakened Machine. No mother. No father. No Ambrose.

I reluctantly climb into the back of the car, dreadfully awaiting the ride home. Once everyone has found their seat, Orville starts driving. I didn't realize how long we had been there with the Machine. The sky is darkening already. The time with the Machine again felt short, and I think I should have done more for him. He is alone and still lost. All I did was patch him and leave.

"Who's ringin'?" asks Orville. His voice cuts through my thoughts.

"Oh! It's my phone," Marc pulls his cell phone from his right pocket, its ringer becoming louder. "Hi, Angelica. Wait, wait, hold on. He's here, I'll put you on speaker."

"Luca, can you hear me?" The second her voice comes through, I know something is wrong.

"I'm here. What's wrong?"

"I don't know how to tell you this...but, um, they have your grandmother. I came over to check on her and there was a note on the kitchen counter that she wrote. She knew they were coming, Luca. I wondered why she sent everyone away when you all left. I should have stayed."

"Who has her? Lumos?" Panic shoots through me, it's sharp and overwhelming. My heart stutters, missing beats. My palms are slick with sweat. I can't lose her. Not her, too.

"Yes, Lumos. They took her! I'm so sorry, Luca."

"It's okay, it's not your fault, Angelica. We are heading back now. We will find her."

"Hurry!" Her voice is trembling. "They are going to execute her tomorrow in Monument Square!"

Chapter 8

She wrote a letter. It may very well be all I have left of my grandmother. I'm sitting alone in my room while Violet gathers everyone downstairs. My fingers tremble as I unfold the letter. The edges of the paper are worn and soft.

"Dear Luca," I start to read Helen's letter. "I know you must be very confused. This whole situation has happened so quickly. I'm sorry I wasn't more candid with you. I did what your mother thought best, and, at the time, I agreed. But now, I see that protecting you may not have had to mean excluding you from everything. Finding the Machine has been a struggle, but I've seen you flourish amongst these new challenges. There is so much you have yet to learn, and I'm afraid I won't be there to teach you. I was wrong to send everyone away. We can't stand down to Chu and let him ruin the Oasis. If we go down, don't go down without a fight. Gather who you can, Luca. Lead them. I know you can."

I sit quietly on the edge of my bed, staring at the signature at the bottom. "Love, Gigi." I am not crying, but I can feel the sensation building behind my eyes. My hands are shaking, but the rest of me feels unnervingly calm. I can't describe how I'm feeling. It's not quite grief. This is something new.

There's a knock on the door. I don't look up from the letter or respond. After a second, the door creaks open and someone walks into the room. From the corner of my eye, I recognize the worn-out color-block sneakers that Ambrose always wears.

My mouth opens, but nothing comes out. Familiar feelings rush in. Anger rises first, followed by regret. After what I did…why is he still here? I don't deserve his kindness, let alone a second chance.

"I'm sorry," it's all I can say before my voice cuts out.

Ambrose sits next to me on the bed. I can see out of the corner of my eye that he is carrying a box, but I still can't look away from the letter. Ambrose places a hand on my thigh. His touch sends a warmth through me. I hadn't realized how cold I had become. Slowly, I let go of the letter and rest my hand on his. That's when the dam breaks and I can no longer hold back the tears. Everything that I have bottled up since leaving the Machine pours out of my eyes. I collapse into Ambrose's chest.

I sob as I relive every emotion of fear, guilt, and loneliness I had been holding in.

What relieves me is when Ambrose pulls me in closer by wrapping his arms around me. His warmth spreads deeper, and as the tears wane, I realize something important. I know that all the pain that has happened in the past can only shape me but it cannot define my future. I won't let it dictate my path forward. I can't dwell on what I did or what was done to me. I must find a way to embrace it and let it go.

"I made this for you," Ambrose says softly. "Violet told me you needed to connect to the Machine out in the desert. It's a good thing you had the idea to leave that long-range communicator with the Machine."

"Why did you do this for me?" My voice is hoarse and my eyes are still red from crying. I feel like a mess.

"Because I love you."

"I love you, too. I'm sorry for what I said."

"I know, Luca."

"How does this work?" I ask, straightening up as Ambrose hands me what he made. It's a wrist gauntlet with an input display.

"It's linked to that communicator you left with the Machine. It allows him to transmit data to you and vice versa. So it is essentially like you never left the desert."

"Ambrose, I can't thank you enough for this."

"Don't mention it. It's why I am a part of the team."

"You're more than just a part of the team." I embrace Ambrose in a tight hug.

"Go ahead. Put it on."

I slip the gauntlet over my left hand. The device is metallic gold with an irregular display. It's pieced together with whatever Ambrose could find, yet it came out looking as though one of the factories manufactured it. The display connects to a black sleeve with fingerless gloves.

"And the Machine can hear you so you don't have to type things out. It's speech-to-text," Ambrose is beaming over his creation, and rightly so.

Once it's fit into place, I feel a buzz from the gauntlet. I look down and notice I have a message. It's the Machine.

"I won't let them do to your grandmother what they did to Amelia."

"Then let's get to work." Determination rises in me. I grab Ambrose's hand and lead him downstairs to join the rest of the group.

"Luca! I'm glad you came down. Everyone is almost here," says Violet as Ambrose and I reach the end of the stairs. I see Angelica, Orville, Marc, Jasmine, and the Sweeneys. Everyone except Willow. I swallow a lump in my throat, worried she's not coming. Maybe she decided to go underground after all.

"Willow?" I ask.

"She's running late, but don't worry about her. She's bringing a couple of friends!" says Violet.

A wave of relief washes over me. I can't believe all these people showed up for my grandmother even after she sent them away.

"Oh! Here she is now." Willow walks in the door with her husband, Jeffrey, and two others I recognize from the night Chu executed those people in the square.

But even with these people, I am afraid it won't be enough to overthrow Chu and displace Lumos. We need more help. I just don't know who to trust.

"So what do we know?" asks Willow.

"Helen is being held at the Oasis Response control room in Purple," Violet replies.

"And the control room is heavily guarded by Oasis Response members," adds Jasmine. "More so than Monument Square seemed to be the other night."

"So we would have better odds there," says Willow.

"Chu plans to execute Helen in the morning," Violet says grimly. "He's likely going to make a spectacle out of the execution and broadcast it to the Oasis like he did the first time."

"Could that work to our advantage?" asks Jeffrey. "If it's being televised, we could get our message to the whole Oasis, not just those present."

"The problem isn't getting our message out," I say. "It's being able to overcome Lumos and beat Chu which, at this moment, we don't have enough manpower. Especially since we don't have the support of the drifters."

"So doing this plan alone will likely be a suicide mission," adds Ambrose. He said exactly what I was thinking but was too scared to say out loud. His words sink into the room. Everyone goes quiet. The weight of this mission just became real for everybody.

"We have to at least try to save Helen," Violet says firmly. "At any costs." Everyone nods in silent agreement. I didn't realize how committed they were, not just to the Oasis, but to my family, the Machine, and the cause. But I am happy I have them by my side. It strengthens my resolve.

"There is more discontent with Chu than you may realize," Angelica speaks up. "I believe all it the Oasis is on the verge of rebellion. It just needs a spark."

"What about Chu's story that Lumos was taken care of? That he is a savior of the people?" asks Marc.

"Not very many people seem to have bought his antics," continues Angelica. "The only thing it did do was cement fear in the eyes of the people. Essentially keeping them quiet and complacent, too, just not how he intended it to happen. Fear keeps them in line. It's not loyalty – it's survival.

"Everyone is worried they could be next," Ambrose adds.

"Exactly."

"We can't just go in without any sort of weapons, right?" I ask, my voice steady but tense.

"I can get us some stun rifles," says Orville. "It won't be a match for their real guns, but at least it will provide us with some cover."

"Better than nothing. Everyone should go home and get some rest. Meet back here at daybreak. We will head to Monument Square and put an end to this madness Chu created," I say. My voice comes out firmer than I feel.

After people start to leave, dread sets in. *What if I am leading them straight to their deaths? What if this is all for nothing?* No. I can't think like that. My grandmother is counting on us. On me.

"Ambrose, Violet? Can you help me with something first before you leave?"

"What's up?" asks Ambrose.

"I've been thinking since you gave me this gauntlet that maybe we could use it to give the Machine some more processing power. Connect his signal to another computer."

"Yeah, I think that could work actually." Ambrose's eyes light up.

"Great, let's go down and connect him to the holo map table. It has the most processing power out of anything in this house."

"Sounds like a great idea to me," says Violet. "He might be

able to assist us more effectively."

"And I hate to ask this, but could you two stay here with me tonight?" My voice falters, but they don't hesitate to respond.

"Of course," they say in unison.

Chapter 9

"Welcome and thank you for turning your attention to Monument Square once again." Chu's voice booms over the loudspeakers. His words slice through the tense air. Cameras scan the entire plaza broadcasting the spectacle to every corner of the Oasis, just as Violet predicted. Whether or not we have the Machine or the drifters on our side, today is the day we make our stand.

"You may be wondering why we have made such a production of this event. Or why I have even asked you here today," Chu says from the podium on stage. "But today, I bring forth Helen Juniper, another rebel captured and brought to justice. But she isn't just any rebel. She's the leader of the second group terrorizing our sacred Oasis. While we haven't captured every member of her little cabal, we believe that with her death we can snuff out her weak and demoralized rebellion. Her end will mark the beginning of a new era for the Oasis. An era free from the terror of living beneath an artificial intelligence and from these rebels that wish us harm."

"Everyone ready? Once we make our move, there's no turning back," Orville's voice crackles to life over the communicator in my ear. The weight of his words settles heavily on my shoulders. The gathered crowd feels suffocating as I stand among them, trying to blend in. I pull the hood of my black jacket lower over my face and duck my head down hoping to remain hidden.

I spot Ambrose from across the crowd. He and Violet came along with me to scope out Monument Square as people began to show up. There is a suspicious lack of security, which means one of two things. Either this whole thing is a trap, or Chu doesn't believe we'd dare make a move as bold as what we have planned. I pray it's the latter.

Our plan is simple but risky. Willow, her husband, and their team are working on infiltrating into the communications trailer Chu set up in order to broadcast the execution live across the entire Oasis. Basically, he isn't relying on the news to cover this story. Willow's team's goal is to ensure the broadcast continues no matter what happens so that our message gets out. Meanwhile, Angelica and the Sweeneys are sowing seeds of doubt in the crowd, whispering that Chu is lying and that he should be feared. The goal is to make the people believe we are here their allies, not enemies. Those of us hidden in the crowd have stun pistols tucked into our waists. Marc and Orville are around the corner armed with rifles to help cover us as we storm the stage. We are waiting for Chu to bring my grandmother out on stage before we move. We have to make sure she is here and this is not a trap.

As I scan the crowd for Violet, I see one of Chu's Oasis Response cadets hurry to him at the podium and whisper something in his ear. Chu's polished demeanor falters slightly before the cadet marches back offstage. Chu looks slightly thrown off his game.

"Everyone, please. You will have to excuse me for just a moment," Chu says and then steps away from the microphone.

"Uhhh, does anybody know what's going on?" asks Ambrose over the comms.

"Chu is arguing with some cadets backstage," Willow replies. "I can't hear what they are saying from here."

"Any eyes on my grandmother yet?"

"Not yet," come the responses, one after another.

"Okay. As soon as you do, we make our move. Willow, have you guys wired into the communications trailer yet?" Anxiety grows inside me. What is taking Chu so long to return?

"Give us five more minutes. We almost have everything in

position."

"Keep an eye on Chu," Violet's voice cuts in. "He's coming back."

"Thank you for waiting," Chu steps back to the podium with a visibly strained smile. "It seems we have created quite a stir with today's proceedings. None of my Oasis Response cadets have located any rebels among us. However, we did encounter a minor inconvenience of tampering with our communications. It was a remote attack on our system with no clear objective. But, no matter, we can never be too cautious, can we?"

"Willow, Jeffrey, is everything alright?" I ask, my nerves are fraying.

"We had to make a move from our location but whatever they detected was not us," Jeffrey reassures. "We are safe now, though. Everything is ready. The attack on their systems gave us just the distraction we needed to finish."

"Good. Now all that is left is getting Luca up on that stage," says Ambrose. I still can't believe everyone accepted me as a leader after my grandmother. I hope I can make the same impression on this crowd. *Can I really do this?*

Suddenly, the crowd grows quiet followed by a segment close to the stage erupting in a cacophony of boos, hisses, and scattered cheers. I turn toward the stage trying to figure out what the racket is for. It's my grandmother being dragged onto the stage. Her face is bruised and her eyes are haunted, yet defiant. The sight of her standing there, humiliated in front of these people sends a wave of cold fury through me. Chu has elicited such a disgusting response from these people that they are enthralled by this execution.

"Helen is on stage," Violet confirms. "Orville and Marc, get into position. Luca, it's your call."

I'm frozen in place. Every muscle in my body locks up as I watch my grandmother march to the center of the stage blindfolded, I have no idea when to go. Why am I the one in charge? I'm not ready for this. Panic grips me. I have to act. I have to save her, but what if I fail?

I wait until they force her to kneel in the center of the stage. The cadets take off her blindfold, thinking they have won. That is the moment I'm looking for.

"Now!" I scream.

Shots ring out as Marc and Orville fire their stun rifles from behind the crowd, dropping the three cadets surrounding Helen. Ambrose, Violet, and I bolt toward the stage, weaving through the chaos. I draw my stun pistol from beneath my shirt, its unfamiliar weight cold and foreign in my trembling hands. I am ready.

I spot an opening to the stage that has been left unguarded. Most of the cadets are distracted looking for Marc and Orville after they fired the original shots. I look at my grandmother on stage. Her cheeks are streaked with tears. I have to reach her. I sprint forward with my heart pounding in my ears. I need to get on stage before the cadets come back. Ambrose and Violet are fighting through the confused crowd.

Just as I reach the first step, my foot fails to make contact. A powerful hand grasps my shoulder and yanks me backward. Before I can react, I lose my footing and the cadet slams me to the ground. My knees and elbows hit the pavement hard and gravel bites into my skin. Thankfully, I manage to keep hold of the pistol, but the cadet towering over me is ready to finish me off. I struggle to my knees and lift the pistol with my right hand. *This is it. Make a stand, Luca!* I pull the trigger and the cadet crumbles to the ground as he's hit squarely in the chest.

Ignoring the pain, I scramble to my feet, brush the pebbles off my knees, and dash on stage. I see my team among the crowd. Angelica and the Sweeneys are maintaining peace in the plaza. The people need to be here until the end. Ambrose and Violet are still working toward the stage it seems the crowd is clearing a path now. I see Willow give a thumbs-up from near the communications trailer. Helen looks up, her eyes filled with disbelief.

"Are you alright? Did they hurt you?" I ask breathlessly as I pull Helen into my arms.

"No, no. I'm fine, Luca, just tied up. Bless you all for coming to my rescue. I'm sorry I gave up hope."

"Don't apologize. It's been challenging for all of us. Let's get you out of here."

Ambrose and Violet are already untying her. Once she's free, they help her off the stage, leaving me alone in the spotlight. Now it's my turn.

"People!" I turn to the crowd. My voice echoes through the square, carried by the microphone at the podium. Some of those who aren't paying attention are now turning toward me, others are pointing. "Can't you see you are being lied to? In the past six months, more innocent lives have been lost since before Calamity! And it wasn't because of the Machine! It was Lumos, lead by Chu. They are who destroyed the plazas and poisoned the Machine to turn him against you! Lumos has been after the Oasis, the Machine, and my family for decades. They are the ones that live in fear of a system that was working! Now, they are spreading all that fear onto you. Never before would we have gathered here at Monument Square to watch an execution. Especially without knowing the absolute truth. Are we going to stand by and let Lumos continue its reign of terror?" I really hope Willow is broadcasting this.

More faces turn toward me. They look curious, confused, and uncertain. A large murmur erupts from the crowd. I can hear some quiet responses of support. They are listening to me, but am I getting through to them?

"We are the Oasis! Are we going to let Lumos keep us in

fear? To keep tearing our society apart? We can no longer live in fear! They are responsible for everything that has happened. Lumos murdered five innocent people on stage here in an attempt to separate themselves from *themselves*. Not to mention all the lives we lost during the Earth Day attack. Don't let fear dictate your life."

I take a pause.

"So I plead you. Believe in the Machine! Renounce Lumos! Help me fight for our home!"

"Luca!" Ambrose's voice cuts through my rallying cry. He's frantic and is flailing his arms, I think to get me off stage. But why? The cadets are either gone or stunned, aren't they? What could he want? Why didn't he just come on stage to tell me?

Suddenly, a sharp, cold pain slices through my back. I stumble forward and gasp as my vision blurs. My legs give way beneath me. I have been shot. I think by a real gun, though I have no knowledge of what it would feel like. My body grows heavy as the world fades around me. I stiffen and crumble to the floor. I feel that I failed. Failed everyone who supported me and my family. I couldn't do enough. I made a mistake.

"Should have known she couldn't keep you out of it forever," a familiar voice sneers. It's Chu. His face comes into view as I lay collapsed on the stage. "Thank you for bringing the rest of your team right to me." His voice is the last I hear before I succumb to the darkness.

Chapter 10

//memory_log_08292038_kindergarten >> 01:23:15 >> replay.exe

Luca grabs his bookbag from the rack by the door. His eyes are bright with excitement. So full of life. His body is practically buzzing with energy. All because today is his first day of school.

He lives with Helen now. It's been a year since Amelia died and everything has changed. Lumos's power grew beyond what I envisioned. I was too slow to stop them. They were tired of always being outmaneuvered by Amelia, so Lumos took her out of the picture. Permanently.

Helen was devastated. She broke down for months because

her heart was obliterated by the loss of her daughter. It has only been recently that she got back on her feet. She's finding new hope as she watches Luca prepare for school. This was Amelia's favorite time growing up and Helen sees her daughter in Luca's similar enthusiasm.

"Luca, slow down!" Helen calls and rushes after her young grandson.

"The first one to the car is the winner!" Luca hollers back, laughing. His backpack slaps against his back as he runs. "I win!"

"Indeed you did," Helen breathes as she catches up to Luca who is climbing into the backseat. "Don't forget, make sure you are buckled up now."

"I won't forget, Gigi."

As the car pulls out of the driveway, Helen looks back admirably at Luca through the rearview mirror. Her heart swells with love and pride. He is a perfect blend of Amelia and Ross – full of courage, life, and a little mischief. She thinks Luca has gotten the best qualities of both of his parents. But every time she looks at him, she's also reminded of everything they've lost. The world is darker with Amelia and Ross, and Helen feels the weight of that darkness every day.

"Are you excited for today?"

"Oh, I am so excited!" Luca giggles, bouncing in his seat. "I can't wait."

"Just remember to be safe and be kind to others, okay?"

"Okay, Gigi. I will."

Helen grips the steering wheel tight with white knuckles. She feels uneasy leaving him alone. She knows the teachers will do their best to keep him safe. She knows many of them personally, but she can't shake the feeling that danger is always lurking. She's lived in constant fear ever since Amelia was killed. There's no such thing as being too safe for Helen. She regrets being too lax before. Feeling responsible for Amelia's death has weighed heavily on Helen.

The drive to the school is short. As Helen pulls into the drive, Luca chirps up in the back seat. He's grabbed his backpack and is digging for something in the bottom. He pulls out something folded and colorful.

"Here, Gigi. I made this for you." Luca hands her a drawing. "It's so you don't have to worry about me while I'm at school." Helen unfolds the paper and tears well in her eyes. It's a drawing of her and Luca, hand in hand, surrounded by hearts.

"Oh, Luca, this is so sweet. It's wonderful."

"It's of us," Luca has a beaming smile on his face. "We'll always be together, Gigi."

"I love you, Luca."

"I love you, too! Have a good day!" Luca hops out of the car and races over to the teacher greeting the students. The teacher points him inside and Luca turns back to Helen and waves goodbye one last time before heading into the school building.

Helen watches him go in, her heart in her throat. She wipes a tear from her cheek. She's proud of the kid Luca is becoming, but he's growing up so fast. The world is so dangerous, Helen now knows how close Lumos is to achieving their goal.

Lumos wants me dead and for the Oasis to burn. I've become too acquainted with death, and more bodies keep piling up. How do I stop this from continuing? I can't let them take Luca, too. I need to work out a solution. A steady hum whirs as a silent vow forms. I will stop Lumos no matter what.

//end_memory_log_08292038_kindergarten >> 02:45:16 >> replay.exe

Chapter 11

The first thing I feel is the gauntlet buzzing nonstop on my wrist. It's a pulse of urgency I can't ignore. My body feels like it has been hit by a freight train, every nerve is screaming in agony. Slowly, I open my eyes and the world comes into focus as I regain my bearings. There are gunshots in the distance and chaos still rages around me. At first, I don't remember what just happened. I remember being on stage, rallying the people, and now I'm waking up on the ground. Then, pain. It's sharp and sudden. My left flank feels cool, almost like it's wet. I look down at my side, my fingers brushing a sticky wetness. When I look at my fingers, they are stained crimson red. Blood.

It all rushes back to me in an instant. I was shot by Balo Chu. He caught me off guard and I blacked out from the shock. I try to lift myself from the ground but my body refuses to cooperate. For now, I resign to lying here. More shots echo nearby. My body tenses expecting more pain, but these sound like stun rifles, not live rounds.

There's pressure on my shoulders as someone starts to drag me off stage. My shirt bunches beneath my arms and around my neck. Every tug aggravates the bullet wound on my side sending unbearable, searing pain throughout my abdomen. It helps me remember more.

I was too focused on saving my grandmother that I forgot about Chu. He left the stage and hadn't come back yet. No one on the team had eyes on him after he argued with the cadets behind the stage. When the cadets brought Helen out, it was all I focused on. Everything will be worth it as long as she is safe.

Thankfully, I see Chu lying facedown on the stage as I am dragged away. It seems someone managed to take him down, but I don't know who. Maybe my message did reach some of the people in the crowd. A lot of them knew my grandmother so there's no way they all believe she's the evil mastermind behind some plot to overthrow the Oasis. If my message didn't reach anyone, then all this commotion would have ended by now, leaving just our small team surrounded in the square.

Chu must have suspected we were going to attempt something. He was smart to wait backstage, biding his time for the right moment to strike instead of being on stage when it started. Someone fought back. But who is pulling me?

The world around me is spinning, and my vision is swimming in and out of focus. I muster the strength to tilt my head back to see who is behind me. To my surprise, it's Enzo, the drifter I met in yellow. They came!

"Try to stay calm, Luca. The fight is far from over. It looks like the Machine is trying to make sure you're alive," he says with a chuckle.

I glance down at the gauntlet. The screen is flooded with a frantic stream of messages that don't make sense. They are all from the Machine. His goal was obviously to try to wake me up and not to tell me anything. A sense of relief washes over me. He is alive and is still guiding us.

"What changed your mind?" I gasp. My voice is barely audible through the pain.

"The Machine sent us," Enzo replies as he drags me toward cover. "He cares for you, Luca, unlike anyone else in the Oasis. Honestly, it has been that way since you were born. Plus, Chu never cared for the drifters being so free from the rest of the Oasis. We were bound to be next on his list to subdue."

"Can he walk?" Violet's voice cuts in as she rushes to my side. "We need to get him somewhere safe."

"Yes, I think I can walk. Just help me up," I groan as I struggle to stand. "Is my grandmother safe?"

"She's fine, Luca. The crowd rushed to protect her after

Chu shot you."

I nod weakly. Violet helps me stand up and they guide me across the fight in the square to a building across the street. I'm watching the fight as we cross. Oasis Response Cadets are fighting in every direction – some against people from the crowd and others against each other. It seems our message of resisting Chu and Lumos inspired everyone, not just the crowd that had gathered to watch. I see Orville and Marc firing their stun rifles at a group of cadets in the northeast corner. Others are helping the injured. For the first time, it feels like we might have a chance at winning.

When we get across the street, I spot Jasmine and Ambrose both leading the cause to help tend to the injured. I am glad to see them in good spirits. They will make great leaders. My heart swells with relief when I spot my grandmother sitting in the corner. Her face is pale, but she's alive.

"Help me over there. She should know I am okay," I murmur.

"On it."

"Gigi," I croak. She hadn't looked up until we were standing just a few feet away.

"Oh, Luca! I thought I lost you," Helen gasps, rushing to wrap me in a tight embrace. She sobs into my shoulder.

I smile, the pain momentarily forgotten as I cling to her. "I told you. We'll always be together."

Chapter 12

We hold each other but the pain in my side flares again, and I remember I'm still bleeding from my wound. I'm beginning to feel faint. I can't stay on my feet much longer. I'm sure the adrenaline is starting to wear off.

"I need to sit," I say. Violet helps me down to the bench. I slump back, my body drained of strength.

"Ambrose, over here! Quick!" Violet yells across the room, getting both Ambrose's and Jasmine's attention. They waste no time making their way over to us. Neither of them are medics, though. I'm not sure what they are going to be able to do for me, but right now, they're all I've got.

My vision blurs as they approach, but I notice something metallic hovering beside Ambrose. I'm almost losing consciousness again. Maybe I'm just hallucinating. Just as my vision fades away, I remember what used to be common in the Oasis. Medbots! It's not just my imagination. The Machine – he's back!

The gauntlet buzzes me awake again, and a message flashes across the screen: *I'm sorry I couldn't protect you from injury. My medbots are healing your wound, but you've lost a lot of blood.* The Machine had a plan since before the attack in April. While I could tell that me getting shot was not in the plan he devised, everything else has been by design. Befriending the drifters, finding him out in Yellow, Chu being taken down, and my grandmother being safe. It was all his plan. He just needed some human help for some of it. The Machine is back in a big way, not just through simple messages. He's helping heal the injured. Heal me. If it wasn't for the blood staining my clothes, I could almost forget I was shot. I exhale in relief. The pain is starting to fade as the medbots continue their work knitting my flesh back together.

"Are you feeling okay? You look flush," Ambrose says with a tone of concern. "The medbots are almost done fixing the wound. The bullet went clean through and missed your vital organs."

"I'm feeling better. The pain is less substantial. Is everyone else alright?"

"Nobody else was injured. Willow and her team ensured

that the broadcast remained live to the Oasis. Everyone heard your message and, most importantly, saw Chu shoot you in cold blood."

"I remember seeing Enzo. He dragged me off stage. Did the drifters really come?"

"Yes. The Machine convinced them to come. Their presence in the Oasis was what had Chu so tense. He was arguing with the cadets behind the stage to divert resources to deal with the drifters rather than focus on us here in Monument Square. But the drifters were already past their defenses, which drew everyone back to the square, bringing the fight to us."

"What about Chu? Is Lumos defeated?"

"The drifters are rounding up the remaining Lumos agents," Ambrose replies. "But Chu slipped away through the crowd. Enzo has people looking for him."

"What you need to focus on right now is yourself, Luca," replies Violet, a note of worry flustering their tone. "You are looking very pale still."

"I'm fine, we need to find Chu," my head spins but I want to push through this. I need to see the mission through to the end. I try to stand but my legs give out and Ambrose gently pushes me back down.

"Luca," Ambrose holds me to the seat. I am not strong enough to resist him in my weakened state. Even though he is barely exerting any force, I can't budge an inch. "You've done enough. Let the others take care of this part."

"But Ambrose…" I continue to attempt to resist him yet it is futile. I don't want to stop. I want to see this though. But the truth is, I'm barely holding on. My body is screaming for rest and my mind is fogging over. I adjust my position and lean my head against Ambrose. Looking down, I see the Machine has finished fixing my gunshot wound. Congealed blood stains my clothes. I feel defeated that I can't continue on, but Ambrose is right. "I need to rest," I murmur.

I drift off into a strange pseudo-slumber. I am caught in the space between consciousness and oblivion. Time seems to crawl. In this state, I can't tell if I am slipping into a dream or in the final stages of dying. I feel the presence of everyone around me, but something feels off. My mind is split. Part of me feels detached, almost delusional, while the other part feels calm and at peace. I can't decipher the strangeness of this moment.

Before I let myself drift off further, I glance up at Ambrose to make sure he isn't concerned. He isn't panicking. I see contentment on his face. Despite the worry etched on his face for obvious reasons, there's something else there, too. Accomplishment. Like we have won.

As that realization settles, a wave of resolve washes over me. If Lumos really is defeated, then I can finally rest. Knowing that my mother's work will endure, and the Oasis lives on, is fulfilling, to say the least. I am happy, too. I have saved the Machine and what I hold dear to me. My family, the people I love, are safe and alive. Without them, I would have lost myself in all this madness. But now, I can let go. Even if for only a moment.

Chapter 13

//memory_log_07232037_lastday >> 21:12:36 >> replay.exe

"You'll do great things for this place," Amelia says softly. Her fingers gliding across the keyboard in a dimly lit room. She sits at a computer in an otherwise empty room.

On the screen in front of her, a line of text appears: *Amelia, why have you grown distant with me?*

She hesitates, her eyes darken. "I...I haven't. I've grown to view the world realistically. It isn't as kind as we hoped it would be. People are pissed with what I've built. They are coming for me. So, I need to set realistic expectations. You do, too. When I disappear from the Oasis, don't forget me. Remember me in those I leave behind. For there will come a time when they will need you the most. A time of division where it may get complicated to delineate a clear line between right and wrong, good and evil. But remember me and the lessons we have learned and you will come out to be superior."

I will always remember them. You need to know, Amelia, that you must remain optimistic in light of realism to retain the part of your humanity that makes you who you are. In other words, realism must be tempered with hope. Always remember the many amazing things you created that ensured humanity survived. You and Ross, you created something worth fighting for. Something worth believing in.

Someone suddenly pounds on the door and Amelia's eyes widen. "Open the door, Amelia!"

"It seems it is my time, my friend," She whispers, her voice barely audible. "They have finally found me." She leans closer to the screen that is illuminating her face with a soft glow. "Promise me you'll take care of them when I'm gone. Please keep them safe."

I promise, Amelia. I will.

//memory_log_07232037_lastday >> 21:30:28 >> replay.exe

Chapter 14

ONE YEAR LATER

The Oasis has finally found peace again. After everything that's happened over the last twelve months, I think back to the day I was shot in Monument Square. It feels like a lifetime ago, and in many ways, it was. Things got a bit rocky for the Oasis after that. The shattered peace left the Oasis to reckon with the fallout and we had to decide how to move forward. Lumos had destroyed the core tenants of the Oasis, and stripped away layers of our society revealing ugly truths hidden beneath our utopian façade.

Our first challenge was rebuilding our government. Chu had murdered the Legislative Council, leaving the Oasis leaderless. The Machine was overwhelmed, tasked with tending to the injured and rebuilding the destroyed portions of the Oasis that Lumos had ignored during their six-month reign. Fear lingered like a shadow and many were skeptical; that Lumos was completely stopped. The question that loomed was how do we ensure that Lumos sympathizers don't infiltrate our reformed government and tear everything apart again?

Some argued that the only solution was to relinquish all control to the Machine. But the Machine was never meant to rule over humanity. He was designed with humanity at his core. He was meant to assist us, not dominate our decisions. Others wanted the opposite, a move away from our AI companion entirely, leaving humans to govern without any input from the Machine.

The solution is still up in the air. The Machine, ever-neutral, will support the change that will best serve the Oasis and the people that inhabit it. But, ultimately, he left this decision up to the people to decide.

On the bright side, the Machine has confirmed that all Lumos agents have been apprehended. There might still be those may be people with sympathies to their cause, but no one directly involved in the orchestration of the attack or the coup on the Oasis remains in power.

In one week, the Oasis will host an election for the Legislative Council. This election may perhaps be the most pivotal vote of our generation, one that may reshape the political climate of the home I grew up in. Despite this uncertainty, I remain steadfast in my belief that the Machine has a plan for us and that, no matter the outcome, we will be on the right path forward.

—

Today is a great day. I am in an excellent mood, my outlook is bright, and I feel a deep sense of accomplishment – for my family, for my home, and for everything we've survived. And more than that, today marks the realization of a lifelong dream. I passed the trials and I am becoming the Machine's acolyte.

"Luca!" Ambrose hollers from downstairs. "Are you about ready? We are gonna miss the whole ceremony!"

Ambrose, Violet, and my grandmother are waiting downstairs. I have been in my room since breakfast, preparing for this moment. Being the Machine's acolyte has been my dream since I was young. I just never didn't realize it was my destiny until a year ago.

"Coming!" I call back. I straighten my bowtie one last time as I stare intently into my eyes in the mirror. My reflection gazes back with determination. This is it.

"Looking sharp," compliments Violet. Violet still pursues fashion, but they have since taken a job in Purple with Oasis Response handling operations logistics. Violet and Jasmine practically run the department now. I have learned one thing about Violet over the years, and it's that they have a keen ability of being a natural-born leader.

Ambrose, on the other hand, is still his goofy self. He still cracks jokes to cheer me up, even after a long day of working in the greenhouses. He's been my rock through it all, even after our falling out. I am so grateful we resolved our argument and that he gave me a second chance after I made such a rash decision pushing him away.

As for my grandmother, Helen has officially retired from all official and unofficial duties. Retirement suits her. She looks more at ease these days, though I am sure she misses the action. Lumos took a lot from her, and she has earned some rest.

While the Oasis took its time healing from the events of the attack and the aftermath, the Machine sparred no time in restoring the physical infrastructure. The O.A.I.T.s are back online, RAMON has some new upgrades to the stations and monorails, and most importantly, the Tree has been rebuilt. It was the final piece of the puzzle and took nearly the entire year to accomplish, but it's finally standing tall again as the symbol of the Oasis. And today, I begin my work alongside the Machine, just like my mother before me.

When we arrive at the base of the Tree, a large crowd has already assembled in front of the stage for the ceremony. It fills me with pride seeing so many people enthusiastic about the Machine. I worried that Lumos had done too much irreparable damage, that people would hate the Machine. But instead, it seems the Machine has become more than just a tool. He's a member of our family, just as integral to the Oasis as any one of us.

The ceremony is brief. Some guests exchanged remarks about perseverance and fortitude. It was an interesting topic, though I barely register their words. My thoughts are distracted thinking about the Machine, and by everything we've endured to get here. A year ago, I was at my lowest. I thought I had lost everything that I held dear to me. But now, as I stand on this stage, waving to a crowd of people excited for the future of the Oasis, I realize how far we've come. With my family at my side, I am ready to conquer whatever comes next.

And with that, I am complete.

Acknowledgments

This story has been over six years in the making. While Luca's story has reached its conclusion, I may just have some more aspects of the world of the Oasis to share. So, please stay tuned to my social media for my future projects.

This past year has been a challenging time and was full of exhaustion, turmoil, and confusion. But writing this story was also at the heart of my journey. It brought me so much joy to write, and I am so glad to finally get to share it with you.

Again, I want to thank my sister, Krayton Koski, for taking time out of her schedule to be the first person to read Luca's entire story. Her support means so much to me.

My partner, Giovanni, also deserves a big thank you. He was a part of my editing process for this novella and provided a ton of insightful edits and suggestions to improve my writing.

Finally, I am so thankful for my cover designer, Bailey Hansmeyer, who created another stunning cover for Reboot.EXE. It's cohesive but also unique, and it's a perfect match for what I had envisioned. Thank you for bringing my writing to life through your graphics.